Papa, Daddy, & Riley

BY SEAMUS KIRST

ILLUSTRATED BY DEVON HOLZWARTH

Magination Press • Washington, DC • American Psychological Association

To the daddies, papas, mommies, mamas, and everyone else who has ever made a child feel loved —*SK*

For the Gibbs Family —*DH*

Books for Kids From the
American Psychological Association

Copyright © 2020 by Seamus Kirst. Illustrations copyright © 2020 by Devon Holzwarth. Published by Magination Press, an imprint of the American Psychological Association. All rights reserved. Except as permitted under the United States Copyright Act of 1976, no part of this publication may be reproduced or distributed in any form or by any means, or stored in a database or retrieval system, without the prior written permission of the publisher.

Magination Press is a registered trademark of the American Psychological Association. Order books at maginationpress.org, or call 1-800-374-2721.

Book design by Gwen Grafft

Printed by Sonic Media Solutions, Inc., Medford, NY

Library of Congress Cataloging-in-Publication Data
Names: Kirst, Seamus, author. | Holzwarth, Devon, illustrator.
Title: Papa, Daddy, and Riley / by Seamus Kirst ; illustrated by Devon Holzwarth.
Description: [Washington, D.C.] : Magination Press, an imprint of the American Psychological Association, [2020] | Audience: Ages 4-8. | Summary: When a classmate insists a family must have a mother and a father, Riley fears she will have to choose between Papa and Daddy until her fathers assure her that love makes a family.
Identifiers: LCCN 2019037062 | ISBN 9781433832390 (hardcover)
Subjects: CYAC: Families—Fiction. | Gay fathers—Fiction.
Classification: LCC PZ7.1.K626 Pap 2020 | DDC [E]—dc23
LC record available at https://lccn.loc.gov/2019037062

Manufactured in the United States of America
10 9 8 7 6 5 4 3 2 1

On the first day of school,
my parents walked me
to my classroom.

My friends were being
dropped off by
their families, too.

Olive was with her mom and dad.

Molly was with her mom.

Hector was with his grandma.

Luke was with his
foster mother.

I was with my dads.

"I love you, my little princess."

"I love you, my little dragon."

When the bell rang, I hugged Papa and Daddy goodbye.

"I love you, Papa and Daddy!"

"Hi, Olive!"

"Hi, Riley! Who are they?"

"Those are my dads!"

"You have two?
But which one is your *dad* dad?
And where is your mom?"

"They are both my dads," I answered.
"My belly mommy doesn't live with us."

"One mom and one dad make a baby,
and that makes a family," said Olive.
"So which dad is the *real* dad?"

I was confused.

If a family only has one dad, did I have to pick one?
Was I Papa's princess, or Daddy's dragon?

I had seen a picture of the
belly mommy who gave birth to me.

I look like her, but I also
look like Papa and Daddy.

I have black hair,
just like Daddy.

And I have freckles
on my nose,
just like Papa.

And I like to shoot hoops,
just like Papa.

I like to bake cookies,
just like Daddy.

I'm a good swimmer,
just like Daddy.

And I'm a good singer,
just like Papa.

I love painting
colorful pictures,
just like Papa.

And I love playing
with dogs and cats,
just like Daddy.

I thought all day, but I just couldn't figure out who my *real* dad was!

When Papa and Daddy came to pick me up,
I was so upset. They noticed right away.

"What's wrong?" asked Daddy. Papa gave me a big hug.

"Olive said families only have one dad!" I wailed.
"But I love having you both!"

"Oh, Riley," said Papa.

I don't want to have to choose!

"Sweet Riley," said Daddy, "you don't have to choose. Some families have one parent, and some have two. Some families have stepparents, or aunts and uncles, or grandparents."

"Neither of us gave birth to you, Riley," said Papa, "but we carried you in our hearts."

"We belong together," said Daddy.

"But what makes a family
a family, if every family is
so different?" I asked.

"LOVE,"

said Daddy.
"Love makes a family."

"Well, I love you both!
So you are both
my real dads."

"That's right," said Daddy.
"You're Papa's princess."

"And Daddy's dragon!"
Papa added. "Roar!"

"And you are Riley's Papa
and Riley's Daddy."

Forever and ever
and always.

About the Author

Seamus Kirst has always loved reading picture books and is still in slight disbelief he has published one of his own. He is absolutely honored to be able to contribute to LGBTQ representation that he wished he could have read and seen when he was young. Seamus is a progressive political writer and the author of another book that's title is probably not a word you want your children to read. His writing has appeared in publications including *The Washington Post*, *The New York Times*, *The Guardian*, *Teen Vogue*, and *The Advocate*. He lives in New York with his two cats, Sugar Baby and Bernie Sanders. Follow him on Twitter and Instagram @SeamusKirst or on Facebook @seamuspatrickkirst.

About the Illustrator

Devon Holzwarth grew up in Panama with the jungle as her garden and parrots and iguanas as pets. Devon earned her BFA in 2000 from the Rhode Island School of Design, focusing on screen printing and painting. Childhood memories and her collection of vintage children's books strongly inspire her work. She currently lives in Aachen, Germany, with her husband, two kids, and beloved old hound dog. Visit her on Instagram @devonholzwarth and at devonholzwarth.com.

About Magination Press

Magination Press is the children's book imprint of the American Psychological Association. Through APA's publications, the association shares with the world mental health expertise and psychological knowledge. Magination Press books reach young readers and their parents and caregivers to make navigating life's challenges a little easier. It's the combined power of psychology and literature that makes a Magination Press book special. Visit www.maginationpress.org.